Sid's Pit

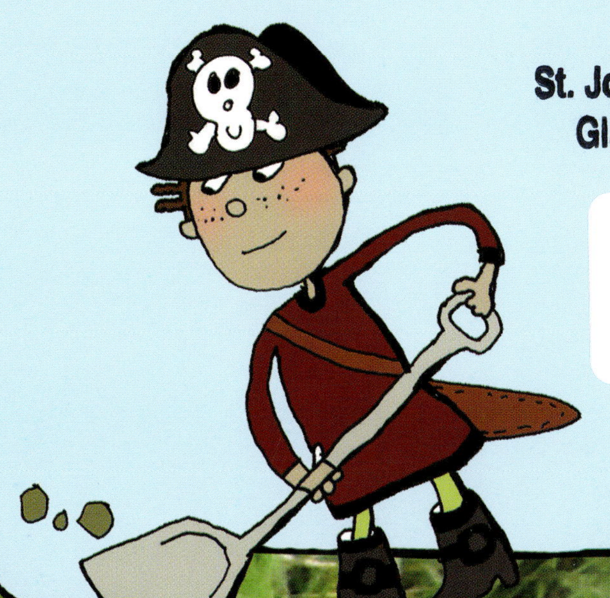

Written by Emma Lynch
Illustrated by Jess Mikhail

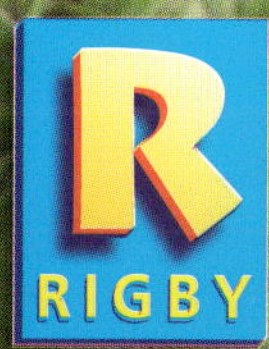

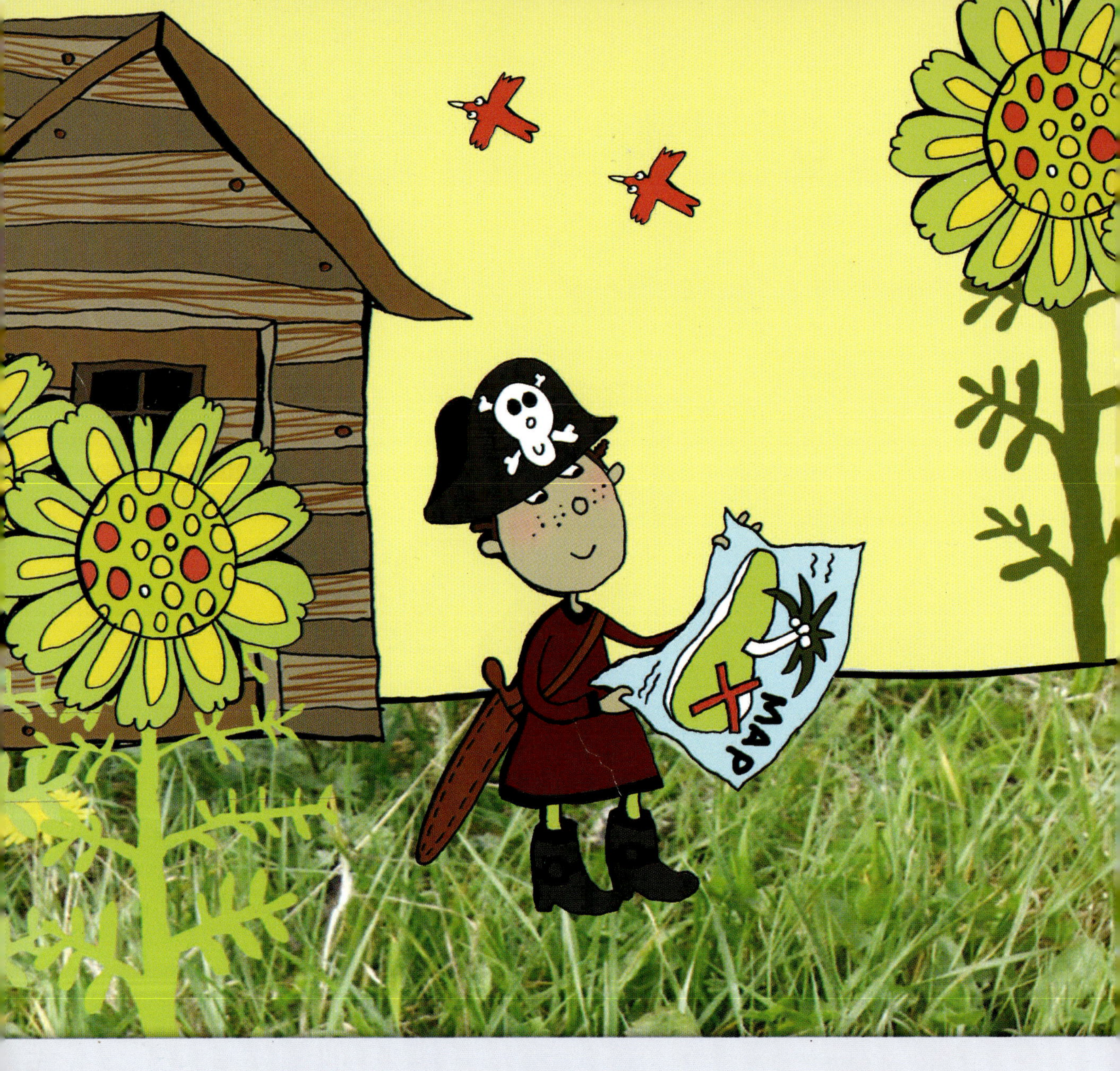

Sid

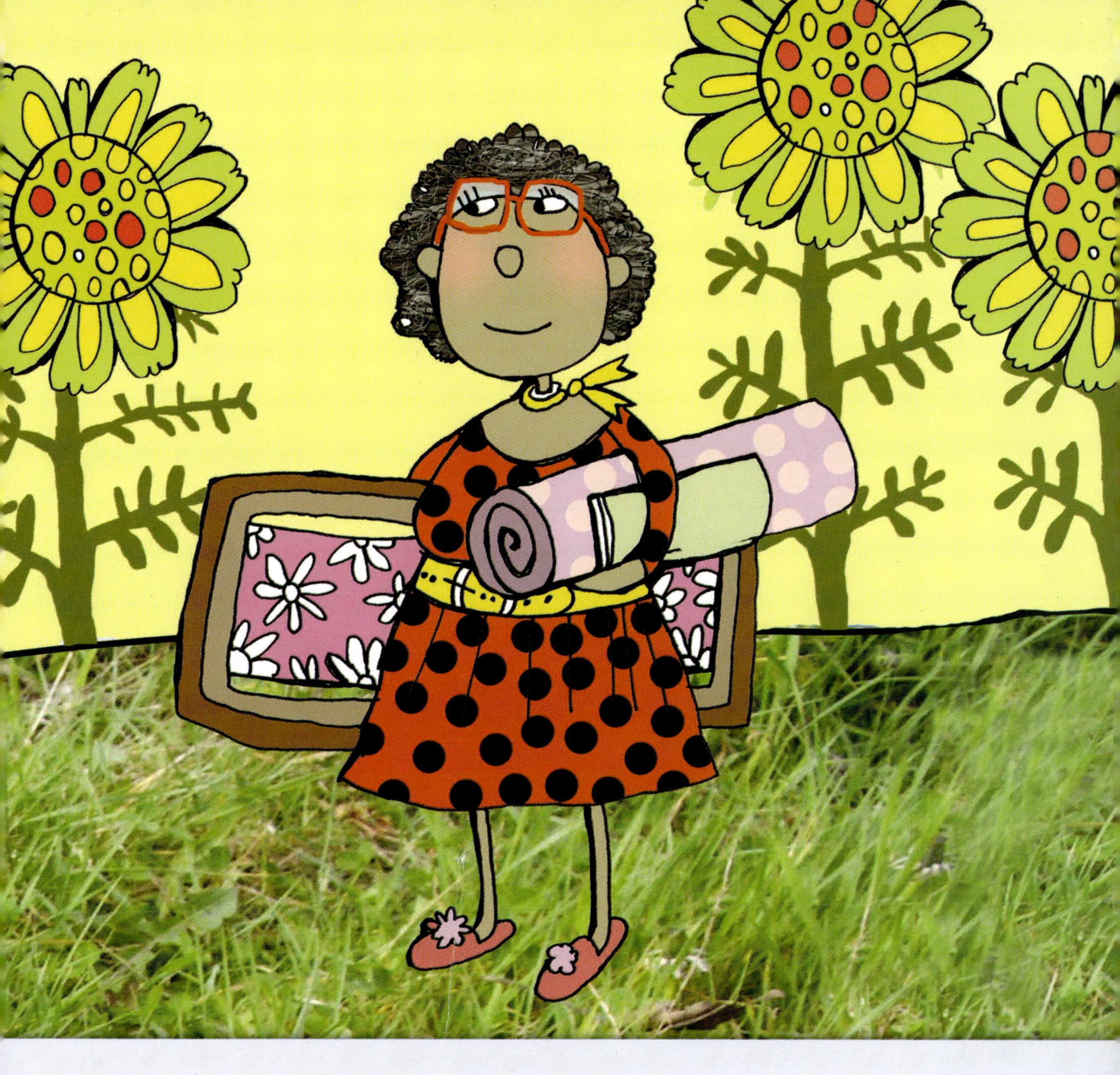

Nan

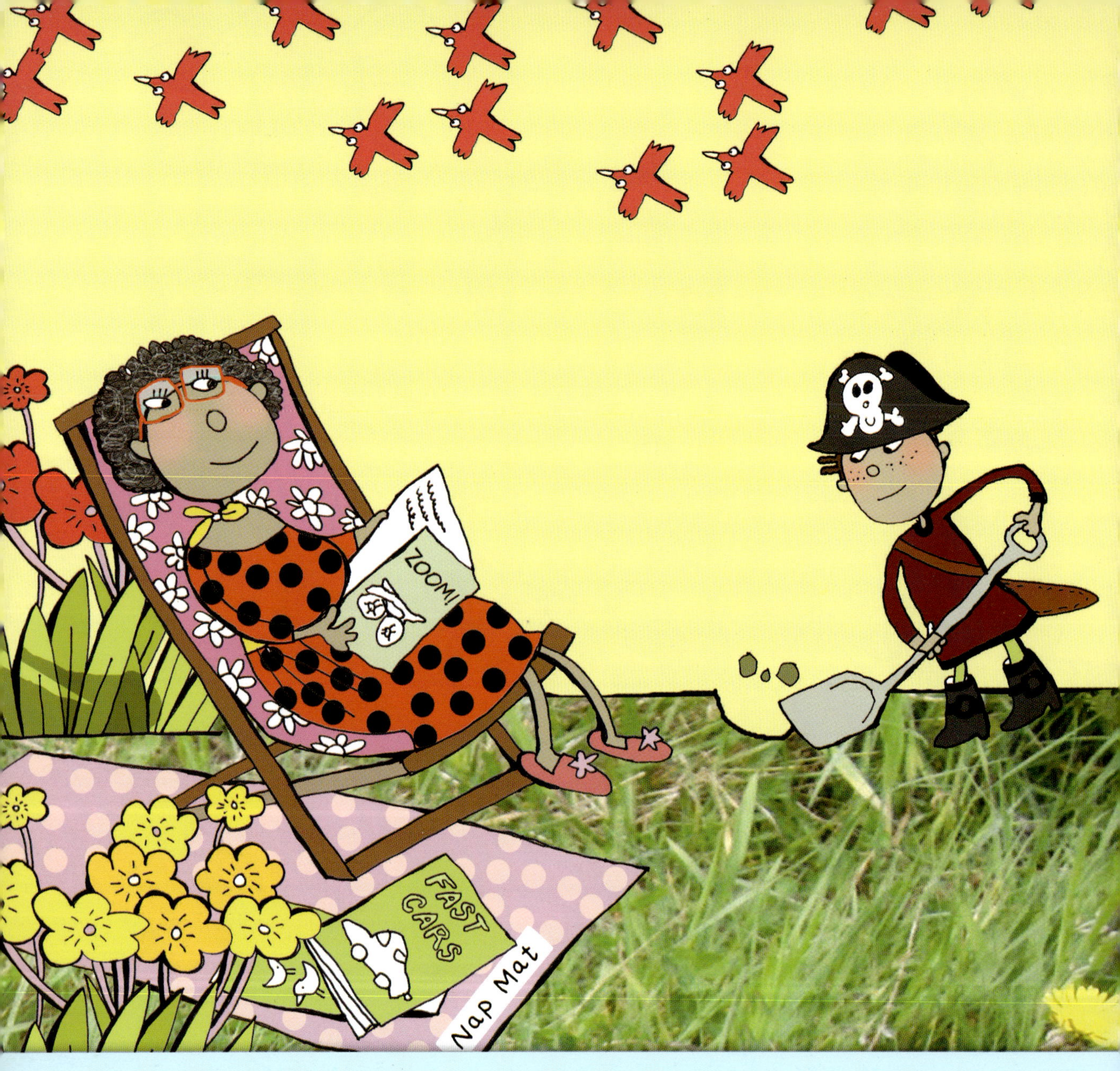

Nan sits.

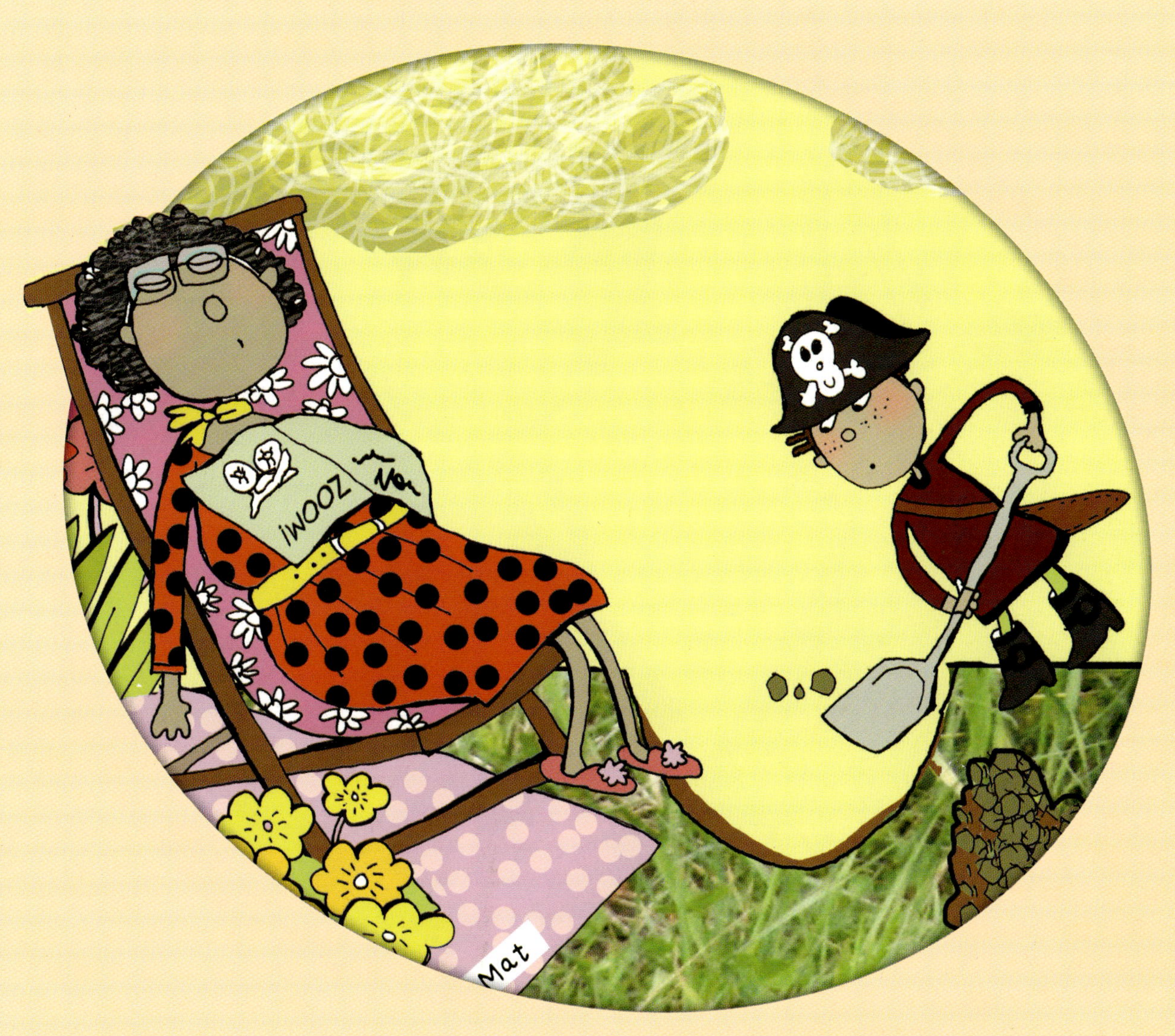

Nan naps.

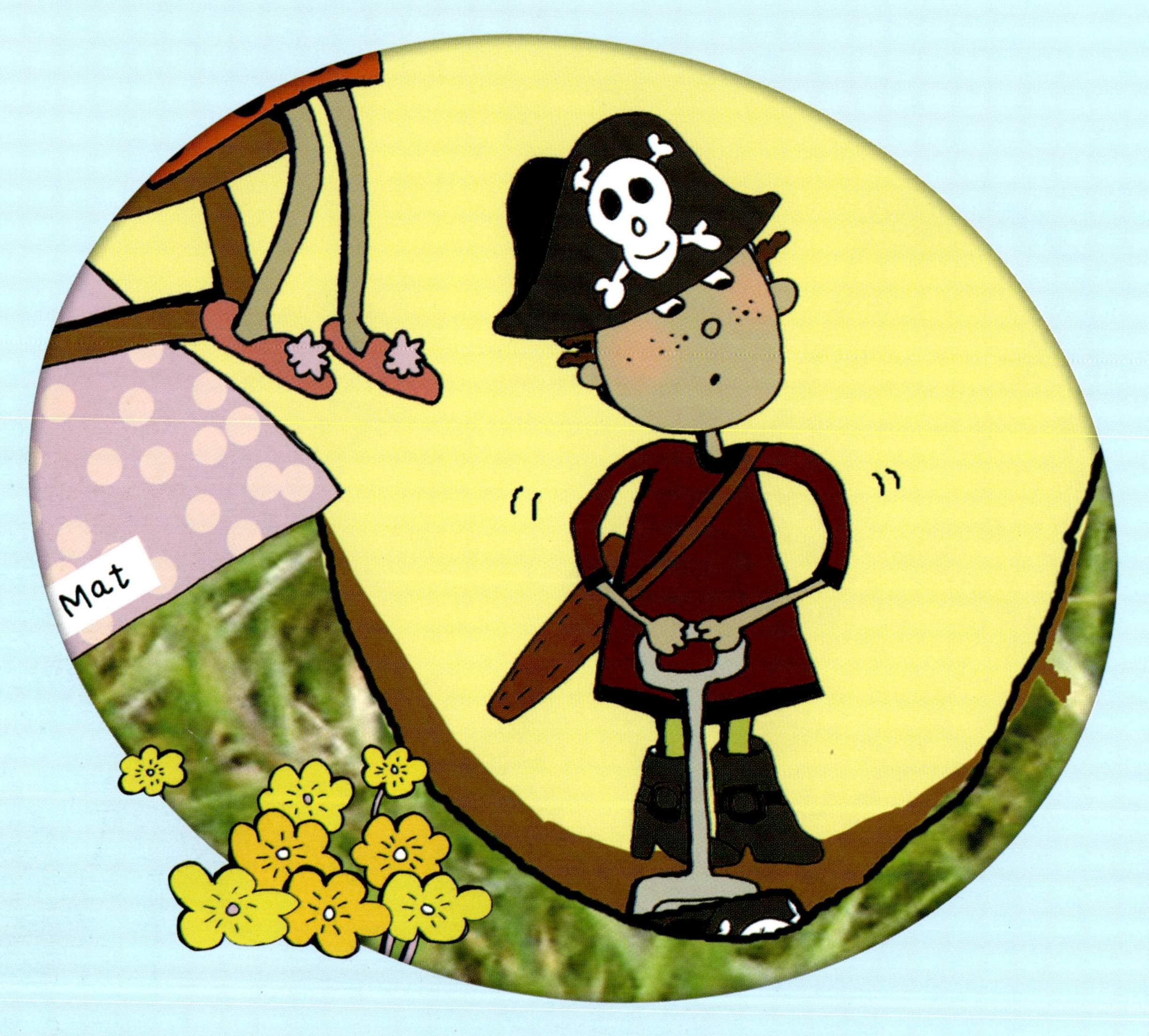

Sid taps a tin.

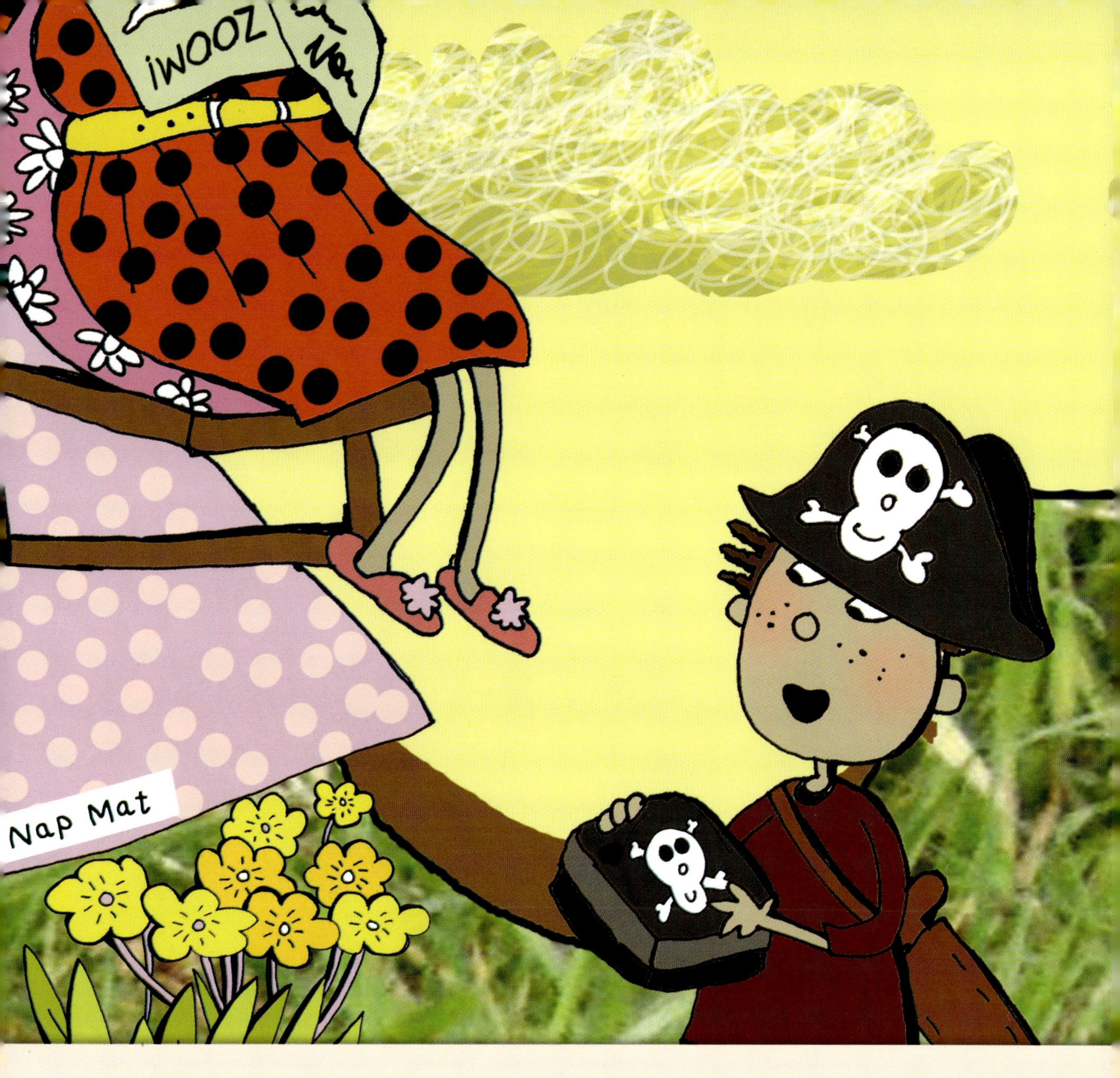

Nan's mat tips!

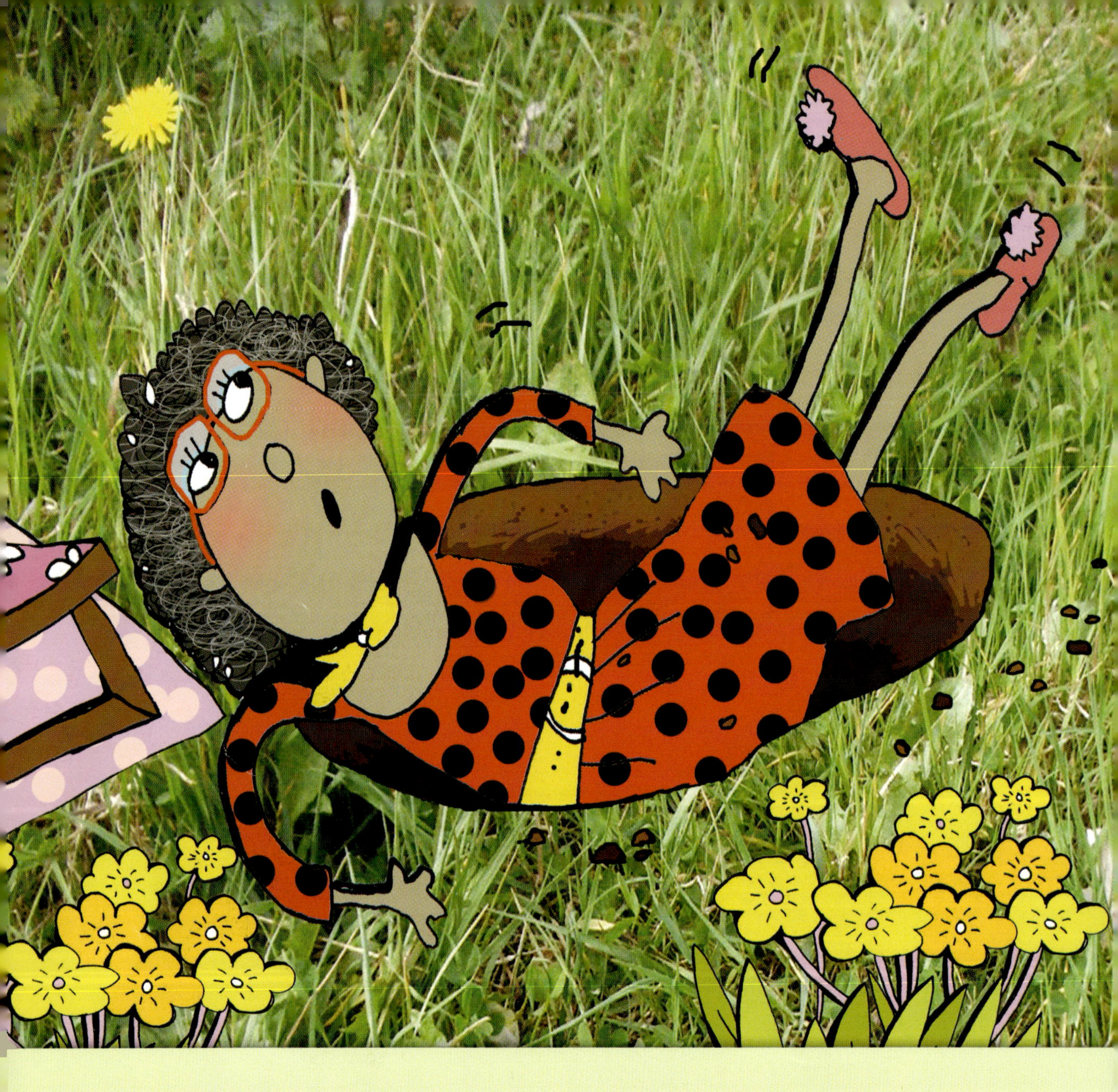

Nan sits in Sid's pit!